Chat, Chat, Chat.

Written by Clare Helen Welsh

Illustrated by Valeria Abatzoglu

Collins

Dad can chat to Nell.

ring

3

Pops can chat with Mum.

buzz

Jax and Nan chat with tablets.

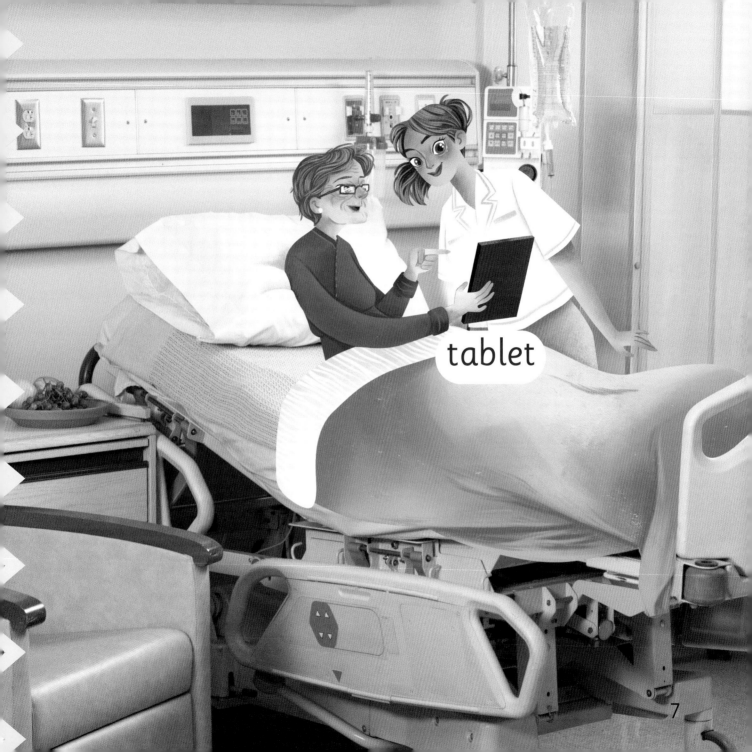

tablet

Viv and Yan chat on laptops.

laptop

I can chat with Ming.

We can all chat!

15

After reading

Letters and Sounds: Phase 3

Word count: 40

Focus phonemes: /j/ /v/ /w/ /x/ /y/ /ch /th/ /ng/ zz

Common exception words: we, to, and, I, all

Curriculum links: Personal, Social and Emotional Development

Early learning goals: Reading: read and understand simple sentences; use phonic knowledge to decode regular words and read them aloud accurately; read some common irregular words

Developing fluency

- Your child may enjoy hearing you read the book.
- Take turns to read a double page, encouraging your child to read labels expressively if they are sounds (**ring** and **buzz**). Read the labels on pages 10 and 11 together, checking your child reads **Bun?** as a question and **Yes!** as an exclamation.

Phonic practice

- Focus on the two-syllable words, and ask your child to clap out the syllables as they read the words slowly. (*tablet/tablets*, *laptop/laptops*)
- Turn to page 10 and challenge your child to identify pairs of letters that make one sound in the words **chat** and **Ming**. (*ch, ng*)
- Look at the "I spy sounds" on pages 14–15 together. Ask your child to find words that contain the sounds /ch/ and /ng/. Prompt them if necessary, e.g. point to the picture on the wall and say: "Cheetah. Cheetah is a /ch/ word." Point to the man in the background and say: "The man is hanging a coat. 'Hanging' is an /ng/ word."

Extending vocabulary

- Focus on the meanings of the words **tablets** and **laptops**. Ask your child:
  - Are they the same or different? How? (e.g. *different – tablets are smaller*)
  - What else might you use tablets and laptops for? (e.g. *play games, read stories*)
- Can your child think of other words to do with technology? (e.g. *phone, washing machine, dishwasher, camera, television*)